To my friends for their hot tea, their stupid jokes,
and their open arms —R. B.

To Lissa —D. D.

First published in the United States in 2009 by Chronicle Books LLC.

Copyright © 2007 by Naïve Livres.
Translation © 2009 by Chronicle Books LLC.
Originally published in France in 2007 by Naïve Livres under the title *Gros Lapin*.
All rights reserved.

North American cover design by Amy E. Achaibou.
Typeset in Neutra Light.
Manufactured in Singapore.

Library of Congress Cataloging-in-Publication Data
Bădescu, Ramona.
[Gros Lapin. English]
Big Rabbit's bad mood / by Ramona Bădescu ; illustrated by Delphine Durand.
p. cm.
Summary: Big Rabbit is in a very bad mood, and though he tries to make it go away, nothing he does seems to work.
ISBN 978-0-8118-6666-8
[1. Mood (Psychology)—Fiction. 2. Friendship—Fiction. 3. Rabbits—Fiction. 4. Animals—Fiction.] I. Durand, Delphine, ill.
II. Title.
PZ7.B13775Bi 2009
[E]—dc22
2008025956

10 9 8 7 6 5 4 3 2 1

Chronicle Books LLC
680 Second Street, San Francisco, California 94107

www.chroniclekids.com

BIG RABBIT'S
Bad Mood

By Ramona Bădescu

Illustrated by Delphine Durand

chronicle books · san francisco

Big Rabbit had a mood.

A bad mood.

A big, bad mood that followed him everywhere.

So he called Squirrel.

But Squirrel didn't answer his phone.

Maybe he wasn't home.

Or maybe he had something important to do, something that had nothing to do with Big Rabbit.

Or maybe . . . or maybe he was having tea and cookies.

Yes, maybe he was having tea and cookies with Bear, and they were telling funny stories, stories so funny they wouldn't want to talk to someone with a **big, bad mood!**

And Big Rabbit had a big, bad, hairy mood that stuck to him like glue.

Big Rabbit turned on some music. Some soft, beautiful music.

Big Rabbit listened, listened, lis—

Augh!

What a beastly, greedy, bad mood!

Big Rabbit was tired.

Tired of his tedious, troublesome, bad mood.

CROC!

He turned on the TV.

But there was his bad mood!

The bad mood as a clown!

The bad mood forecasting the weather!

The bad mood selling shampoo!

The bad mood naked!

Make it stop!!!

Big Rabbit went to the kitchen to make a salad. But he couldn't stop thinking about his big, bad mood—lying in **his** living room, on **his** sofa, picking its nose and wiping its boogers on **his** carpet! What a filthy mood!

Big Rabbit couldn't even finish his salad.

Big Rabbit walked around the house, thinking about his mood. There, in the hall, was a picture of his mom. His mom, who made the best pancakes, who told wonderful stories, and who always smelled like springtime, and Big Rabbit thought: **MOMMY!**

Big Rabbit called his mommy.

But his mommy was very, very busy right now. Could she call him back a little later because Big Rabbit could surely understand that she had something very, very important and really, really urgent to finish that couldn't wait so she loved him and would talk to him soon, OK?

Big Rabbit hung up the telephone.

He tried to think of something very, very important, something really, really urgent that couldn't wait . . .

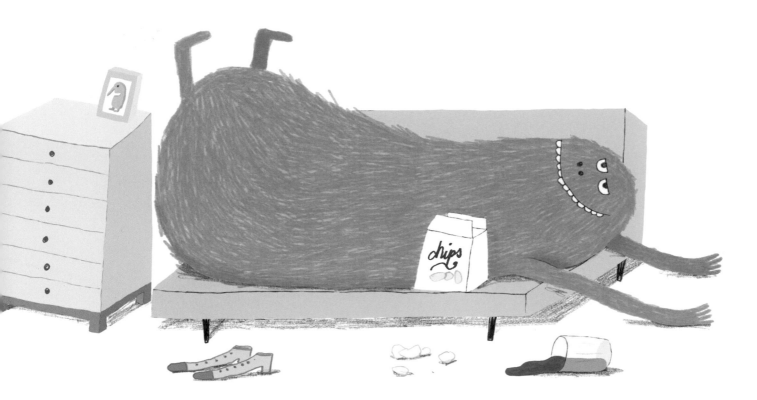

But he couldn't.

He couldn't think of anything but his **BIG,** bad mood, which didn't look like it was going anyplace.

He needed to find a way to make the mood scram, take off, clear out! A way to make the mood leave him **alone!**

Then an idea
came to him—a shining,
brilliant idea! Yes!
Of course!
A path of arrows!
A path of arrows
leading to the door!

Big Rabbit was so relieved,
and so busy moving things out
of the way and drawing arrows,
he didn't even hear
the doorbell ring.

**RINNGG RINNGG
RIIINNNGGG!**

"Finally!" chorused all of Big Rabbit's friends, when Big Rabbit opened the door at last.

There were Squirrel and Bear! And Owl and Anteater and Firefly . . . all his friends! And there, behind them, was his mommy! With a cake made out of pancakes!

And everyone had presents!

Christmas presents?... No, it wasn't Christmas.

Valentine presents?... No, it wasn't Valentine's Day.

Good-bye presents?... No, no good-byes!

"BIRTHDAY presents, silly!"

In the middle of the party, Big Rabbit realized he'd completely forgotten about his bad mood.

Not a hair, not a booger, not a trace. Big Rabbit's bad mood was nowhere to be found. It had disappeared.

And good riddance! thought Big Rabbit.